NITTER PITTER

written by: Stephen Cosgrove
illustrated by: Robin James

A Serendipity Book

ISBN: 0-8431-0570-4 NITTER PITTER

Dedicated to my wife Nancy and her horse called Peter, which is pronounced Pitter; Nancy stays the same.

Stephen

In a burst of sunrise wonder, dawn is born of another day in the meadows of your mind. There are birds of all sorts singing and winging in the early light and all the other animals that live in the meadow begin the day by blinking the mist of morning from their eyes.

The early hush of dawn was broken by the rush of a herd of horses as they raced into the meadow to graze and frolic the day away. There were paints, roans, blacks and bays—horses of every color. The young ones kicked and bucked while the older horses quietly munched the green lush grass of the meadow.

The horses stayed close together as the day wore on. All the horses, that is, except one beautiful stallion called Nitter Pitter. Pitter never played with the other horses because he knew they wouldn't play with him because he was so pretty. He was content to stand on the bluff that overlooked the meadow and watch the antics of the herd below.

"Silly horses!" he nickered, "all they do the whole day through is play and eat, play and eat. I'd never do that silliness, I'm too beautiful to play with that herd of horses!"

With that he wandered farther up the bluff to a special place where the sun hit him just so. Then, if he looked very carefully he could see his magnificent shadow cast upon the ground.

There were times when Nitter Pitter would grow tired of looking at his shadow and would seek other ways to see himself. Almost every day he would rub his soft, silky fur against a rock until it became so shiny that he could see his own reflection. But his favorite of pastimes was to stand near the pond at the end of the meadow and gaze for hours at his mirrored image of beauty on the water.

Occasionally the other horses of the herd would stray close to Pitter but they would ignore him because he was stuck up and he would just put his nose in the air as if they weren't even there.

One warm summer day as Pitter was, as usual, gazing at himself in the water, a friskier than usual colt forgot to look where he was going and quite by accident bumped into the beautiful Nitter Pitter, knocking him into the pond. He looked so silly sitting there with a lily pad draped over one ear that the other horses just whinnied and whinnied and stomped their feet in laughter.

With a lurch and a leap Pitter jumped from the water as the other horses ran back to pastureland meadow. "Dumb old horses!" he thought as he tried to shake himself dry. "They shouldn't laugh at me. Why I'm the most beautiful horse they've ever seen."

He sulked around in the sunshine as he tried to get dry, but he was so wet that the water seemed to cling to him like a sponge. So, with an "Ooomph!" he laid down in the sand at the edge of the pond and rolled and rolled until he was dry.

"Ahhh! That's much better," he said as he trotted around for a moment or two. Then he decided he would have one more look at himself in the pond before he went back to the bluff that overlooked the meadow. As he bent over the water he was shocked to see a scraggly, mud-soaked pony where the magnificent horse used to be. He couldn't believe his eyes, so he looked again and, sure enough, Nitter Pitter had been transformed with a dash of mud here and there into a run-of-the-mill horse with a lily pad hanging from one ear.

"What am I going to do!" he cried. "My favorite thing in all the world was to look at me and now there's nothing to see because I don't want to look at me!" With that he hid sadly beneath a tree and sighed and sighed.

Pitter would have been beneath that tree to this very day if it had not been for a large, black raven who landed on a branch right above his head.

"Hi horse," said the raven, as he settled his wings about him. "Watcha doing?"

"What does it look like I'm doing?" said Pitter with a pout. "I'm hiding because I used to be the most beautiful horse and now I'm just as ugly as can be."

"Well," croaked the raven, "it seems to me that you look just as normal as can be."

"Hmmmph," muttered Pitter, "a lot you know. I used to be so magnificent that the other horses wouldn't even play with me and now that I'm ugly I have nothing to do but hide beneath this tree."

The raven thought for a moment or two and then cawed a little cough and said, "I'll bet you that if you went right now and tried to play with the other horses they wouldn't even know who you were and probably wouldn't care who you are. Then, you wouldn't have to hide any more."

Pitter looked at the raven and mulled it around in his mind and then decided to give it a try.

He shyly ambled out into the meadow and at first the other horses just ignored him. Nitter Pitter was just about to give up when one of the horses dashed by him, nipped him on the shoulder and shouted, "Tag, you're it!"

Pitter was so shocked at being invited to play that he just stood there for a moment. Then, with a whinny, he set out at a gallop to tag another horse.

That day was the funnest day that Pitter had spent in his entire life. He learned how to play hide and seek, and buck and run, and so many other games that were just plain fun. Sometimes, just for the pure joy of it, Nitter Pitter would kick at a butterfly or reach for the sun.

Even after the rains had washed the mud away, making him beautiful again, and amidst all the fun and frolic, Nitter Pitter forgot that he was prettier than all the other horses and remembered, most importantly, that he was just a horse.

When you look into the mirror in the meadows of your mind, remember Nitter Pitter and the lesson he had to find.